COSMO AND THE PIRATES

Daniel Postgate lives in Whitstable, Kent. He has worked as a newspaper cartoonist for many years and more recently has written and illustrated a number of children's books. He likes swimming, walking, cooking and watching the telly.

Daniel Postgate
Cosmo
and the Pirates

PUFFIN BOOKS

To Thomas

PUFFIN BOOKS

Published by the Penguin Group
Penguin Books Ltd, 80 Strand, London WC2R 0RL, England
Penguin Group (USA) Inc., 375 Hudson Street, New York, New York 10014, USA
Penguin Group (Canada), 90 Eglinton Avenue East, Suite 700, Toronto, Ontario, Canada M4P 2Y3
(a division of Pearson Penguin Canada Inc.)
Penguin Ireland, 25 St Stephen's Green, Dublin 2, Ireland (a division of Penguin Books Ltd)
Penguin Group (Australia), 250 Camberwell Road, Camberwell, Victoria 3124, Australia
(a division of Pearson Australia Group Pty Ltd)
Penguin Books India Pvt Ltd, 11 Community Centre, Panchsheel Park, New Delhi – 110 017, India
Penguin Group (NZ), 67 Apollo Drive, Rosedale, North Shore 0632, New Zealand
(a division of Pearson New Zealand Ltd)
Penguin Books (South Africa) (Pty) Ltd, 24 Sturdee Avenue, Rosebank, Johannesburg 2196, South Africa

Penguin Books Ltd, Registered Offices: 80 Strand, London WC2R 0RL, England

puffinbooks.com

First published 2002
006 - 10 9 8 7 6

Printed in Singapore by Star Standard

British Library Cataloguing in Publication Data
A CIP catalogue record for this book is available from the British Library

ISBN 978-0-141-31420-4

Contents

1. Trouble at Mario's

"There's trouble at Mario's pizza restaurant," said Mr Pringle down the phone to Cosmo.

"Spooky trouble?" asked Cosmo.

"Sounds like it," replied Mr Pringle. "Quite a lot of groaning it seems."

"Perhaps there's been too much eating going on," said Cosmo cheekily.

"Perhaps," said Mr Pringle, not really joining in with the joke. "Anyway, I think it's well worth investigating."

"OK, I'm on my way," said Cosmo, and he slammed down the phone.

It had been quite some time since Mr Pringle of the Pricklebourne League of Paranormal Investigation had been in touch with a mission for Cosmo, so Cosmo was thrilled to have something to investigate at last. He pulled on his jacket, mumbled something to his mum and ran off down the road.

It was
winter, and
the afternoon was
cold and already
getting dark when Cosmo
arrived at Mario's place, but the
restaurant was as lit up and
welcoming as a Christmas tree.

The doorbell tinkled as Cosmo
entered, and Mario appeared
grinning from the kitchen.

"Table for one?" he asked.

"No," replied Cosmo. "I'm here
about the groaning."

"Aaaaah!" said Mario. "So you
are the ghost hunter."

"I suppose I am," said Cosmo. "What seems to be the problem?"

Mario waved a finger at the jukebox in the corner of the restaurant, then his eyes widened as he leaned forward and almost in a whisper said, "It's groaning ...

like this …

WOOOAAH!"

"No, no. It's much more of a moan than a groan," said an elderly gentleman at a nearby table. He coughed gently into a napkin. "Like this …

YEEEUUURRR!"

Mario sniffed. "Nonsense. Mine was much better. Just eat your pizza."

"ROOOAAAUUUR!"

"Oh, that one was very good," said Cosmo. "Very scary indeed."

"That," hissed Mario, "was the real thing." All three turned and stared at the jukebox. "And you know what?" continued Mario. "It's not even plugged in."

"Hmm. Objects can often become haunted," said Cosmo matter-of-factly. "Cars, televisions, washing machines."

"Washing machines?!" exclaimed Mario.

"Oh, yes," said Cosmo. "Very common. You know when you empty the washing machine there's always a sock gone missing, never to be found again?"

"Oh, yes," said Mario.

"Phantoms," said Cosmo. He went over to the jukebox and plugged it in. "What we need to do is scare this phantom out of the box," he said.

Cosmo scanned the list of songs on the jukebox, fished a coin from his pocket, pushed it into the slot and pressed some buttons. Suddenly there was the most awful noise imaginable. Everyone covered their ears and grimaced.

"What's THIS?" yelled Mario.

"'CHAINSAW BEAST AND THE STINKERS'. IT'S BEEN AT NUMBER ONE FOR WEEKS," yelled Cosmo.

Suddenly, from out of the jukebox, a tall, skinny pirate leaped,

flailing, into the air and collapsed in
a heap at Mario's feet. Cosmo
quickly unplugged the jukebox and,
looking rather pleased with himself,
said, "That did the trick."

2. Cork-nose Kenny

The pirate clambered on to a chair and shuddered.
"Suffering sea snakes, that was horrible," he gasped.

"PIRATES!" yelled the elderly gentleman, wiping his chin and leaping up. "Leave this to me.

Admiral Blenkinsop of Her Majesty's navy. All hands on deck, call the coastguard, lock him in irons!"

"No, no," cried the pirate, jumping to his feet. "I'm on your side. I'm here to warn you. You're in danger, I'm in danger, we're all in danger, great danger!"

"Danger!" yelled Mario. "Mama mia!" And he started dancing from foot to foot and shouting in Italian.

"Everybody please CALM DOWN!" hollered Cosmo, and the room fell silent. "So, who are you exactly?" Cosmo asked the pirate.

"Cork-nose
Kenny's the name,"
said the pirate, "on
account of my
nose being made
of cork."

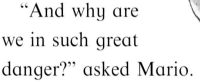

"And why are
we in such great
danger?" asked Mario.

"Ah, now that's a story that takes
some telling," said Kenny, and he
sat back down. "Many, many years
ago I sailed the seven salted seas
aboard a pirate ship. I was the chef
and a proud chef too. I could rustle
up the most mouth-watering meals
from next to nothing. The crew never
went hungry. Even after many
months at sea, when our food rations

had completely gone, I'd boil up the crew's old clothes and make a stew to fill their bellies."

"You ate your clothes?" said Cosmo.

"Oh, yes!" said Kenny. "They were golden days. Then I went and spoiled it all. I decided I'd had enough so I chose to leave. The next

time we were in port I waited until
dark, then sneaked from the ship
and took off into the night with
nothing but the clothes I stood up in
and my captain's leg."

"Your captain's leg?" said Mario.

"Yes. He was Captain
Gingerbeard," continued Kenny,

"the most feared pirate ever to walk the deck of a ship. He could wrestle down a walrus with one arm behind his back and had dogfish for breakfast."

"Great," said Cosmo. "But why are we in danger?"

"Aha!" said Kenny. "I was getting to that part. I took his leg,

so he couldn't come after me, you
see? But once he'd got a new one he
did come after me – from that day
on, he's been on my tail wanting his
old leg back. He's fussy like that.
We're all ghosts now, of course, but
that hasn't stopped him. He and his
ghostly crew have chased me down
through the centuries."

"Was it a wooden leg?" asked the Admiral.

"Yes," said Kenny. "I would have given it back, but I lost it. I've searched long and hard. And now, at last, I've found it."

There was a long silence, finally broken by Cosmo. "So where is it?" he asked.

"There!" yelled Kenny, pointing at a large

wooden thing on one of the tables.

"My giant pepper grinder!" exclaimed Mario.

"Yes," said Kenny. "It used to be his leg. I'd recognize it anywhere!"

"That pepper grinder is my most treasured possession," Mario cried. "No one will take it from me. No one."

Just then, a great wind struck the restaurant, the door flew open and the lights around the windows fizzled and popped.

"He's coming," wailed Kenny. "The captain's coming. We're fish food for sure."

Cosmo slammed the door closed and everyone pressed their faces to the window. Outside, in the darkness, they could see hazy lights – lights from lanterns, lanterns on a great, dark ship.

"How can this be?!" exclaimed Mario. "We're miles from the coast."

"There's no need for sea," cackled Kenny grimly. "Not when you're sailing a *ghost ship*."

3. Gingerbeard!

"**R**ight!" yelled the Admiral. "We are officially at war! I'm taking charge. Man the poop deck. We'll defend this restaurant to the last man!"

"What with?" asked Mario.

"Italian food!" cried the Admiral.

"I don't think food will be much good," said Cosmo.

"Well, what choice have we got?" replied the Admiral. "After all, this is a restaurant."

"Yes, *my* restaurant," clucked Mario. "So *I* should be in charge."

"Maybe we should have a vote on it?" suggested Cosmo.

"No, no, no!" yelled the Admiral. "Don't be daft. I'm the Admiral around here, for goodness' sake ...

I order you to let me be in charge."

"You can't just order us about," said Mario. "It's not fair."

A booming cry came from the darkness outside. "Cork-nose Kenny, I want you!"

Everyone looked nervously at one another.

"OK, you can be in charge," said Mario quickly.

"We're doomed!" wailed Kenny.

"Don't you worry, lad," said the
Admiral. "In all my years at sea I
never lost a man, and I don't intend
to start now!" Then he began
waving his arms about and barking
orders to Cosmo and Mario.

The tables were turned over to
make shields and food from the

kitchen was stacked behind them.
Olive oil was emptied liberally over
the floor to make it slippery and a
large bucket of pizza sauce was
balanced above the door.

"I want you, Cork-nose Kenny!"
came the ghostly cry again, this
time a bit nearer.

Everyone ducked behind the
tables.

"All right, men. This is it," hissed
the Admiral.

"Erm ... I think I should just say
that ghosts can't really be harmed
by things from this world, not
even Italian food," said Cosmo.

"They're often invisible as well, and they can appear and disappear whenever and wherever they choose."

The Admiral stared at Cosmo, then rolled his eyes. "*Now* he tells me," he sighed. "So what on earth do we do?"

"We could talk to Gingerbeard, reason with him," suggested Cosmo. "Kenny could say he was very sorry and Mario could give him his leg back. Then perhaps he'll go away."

"Sounds a bit too easy to me," said the Admiral. "Are you sure a full-on attack won't work?"

"Well, no one can be sure of anything when ghosts are involved," said Cosmo.

"That's good enough for me,"

said the Admiral. He grabbed a
large stick of stale bread and,
swinging it wildly around, he yelled,
"CHARGE!"

The Admiral leaped over the table
and ran at the
door. Slipping
on the olive oil,
he skidded
across the floor,

hit the door and the bucket of pizza sauce emptied over his head. Then, covered in the tomatoey gloop, he fell over backwards and lay there, muttering to himself.

"Not a very good start," said
Mario. "That Admiral's a bit of a
funny old sea dog."

"Did someone say sea dog?" boomed a voice. "That's me. I'm a roaring red sea dog. As crazed as a walrus, as batty as the barnacles in my beard. I want you, Cork-nose Kenny, and I will not rest until I have you!"

4. Flour Power

The voice shook the whole restaurant. There was no doubt about it, Gingerbeard had arrived. Cosmo peeped over the table, but he could see no one.

"You, lad! No point in you hiding like a crab under a rock," boomed

the voice. "There's no getting away
from old Gingerbeard."

Cosmo leaped up, ripped open a
packet of flour and shook it into the
air. The cloud of flour settled, and
there stood the hulking great floury
white figure of a pirate captain,
coughing and cursing. Then Mario
bounded forward, gripping the

pepper grinder.

"My leg, my
leg!" spluttered Gingerbeard.

"Give it to him!" yelled Cosmo.

"I'll give it to him all right," said
Mario, and he started grinding away,
showering Gingerbeard with pepper.

croaked Gingerbeard. He pulled out
his sword and swung it wildly about
while coughing and sneezing and
cursing. It was a terrifying sight.

Suddenly the Admiral was up on
his feet again. He grabbed what was

left of his chilli and anchovy pizza
and slapped it in Gingerbeard's face.

"Anchovies!" Gingerbeard roared.
"I hate anchovies!" Then he
coughed and sneezed
so hard he fell against
the wall and slid
down it.

"Well done, men,"
barked the Admiral.
"That went like
clockwork!"

Gingerbeard lay
slumped on the floor,
silent and still. Then
a new noise came
from him,

a quiet and gentle noise. He was
weeping.

Cosmo, Mario and the Admiral
looked surprised at first, then rather
concerned.

"Give him his leg back,"
whispered Cosmo.

"Of course," said Mario, stepping
forward. "Mr Gingerbeard, don't
cry, I'm sorry. Here ... please, take
your leg back."

"I don't want that bloomin' leg," mumbled the pirate between sobs. "I want Kenny. I want my old mate, my chum, my best pal. All I wanted was to see him again, just for a bit."

Cork-nose Kenny crept out from behind a table. "C-Captain?" he said, almost in a whisper.

Gingerbeard slowly looked up. "Kenny, is that you?"

"Yes, captain," said Kenny.

Gingerbeard rubbed his eyes and pulled the bits of pizza from his beard. Then he sprang to his feet – foot – a great hulking captain of a ghost again. The others stepped back in alarm.

"By the knees of Neptune, it's good to see you!" Gingerbeard roared, and a huge grin appeared from under his beard. Then he swung his arms wide. "Come and give your captain a cuddle."

5. Kenny's Cloth Curry

Gingerbeard gave Kenny such a squeeze that if he had had any life, it would have been squeezed out of him.

"B-but, Captain, aren't you angry?" gasped Kenny.

"I was," said Gingerbeard,

"but not for long. After that I just missed you. But what I really missed most of all was your cooking. No one cooks like our Kenny," he told the others. "You remember that curry you used to make? I used to love that. It was so ... chewy."

"That's because it was made of your clothes," said Kenny.

"I don't care. It was delicious," said Gingerbeard wistfully. "And that crispy bacon – never tasted anything like it since."

"I'm not surprised," said Kenny. "It was your old underpants cut into strips and deep fried."

"And I'm not the only one who missed you," said Gingerbeard with a laugh. "Remember Toothless Pete?"

Suddenly another pirate appeared next to Gingerbeard and gave Kenny a great big toothless grin.

"How could I forget?!" cried Kenny.

"What about Jug-face Terry, Black Jack McDougal, Short Jim Silver and Crayfish Dave?" said Gingerbeard as, one by one, a gang of the most unsavoury-looking characters you could ever imagine appeared from nowhere.

"Yes, yes, yes!" yelled Cork-nose Kenny, who was now in floods of tears, and he hugged each and every one of them.

"It's a bit like *This is Your Life*," said Cosmo.

"Never mind that. Who's going to clear up all this mess?!" exclaimed Mario, looking around at what had

once been his restaurant.

"You leave that to us!" said Gingerbeard. "We'll have this place shipshape in no time."

And before you knew it, Gingerbeard's crew had mopped up all the Italian food, set the tables straight and got everything back to normal.

"Now I'd like to book a table," said Gingerbeard to Mario, "for me and the boys, and you lot too, if you'd care to join us. I can pay handsomely." He pulled a small cloth bag from his pocket and emptied out a number of gold coins on to the table.

Mario stared down at the coins wide-eyed. "Treasure!" he gasped. "I'll get you some menus, sir."

"No, no," roared Gingerbeard. "I don't want any of that Italian muck. I want food – Kenny's food."

"But I don't have any ingredients with me, Captain," said Kenny.

"Don't you worry about that," said Gingerbeard. "Toothless Pete, get the basket!"

Toothless Pete disappeared and
reappeared with a large basket. Out
of it he emptied a pile of old clothes.

"Perfect," said Kenny. He
gathered them up and went into the
kitchen.

Before long, a surprisingly tasty smell filled the restaurant, and Kenny came out proudly holding big bowls of steaming sludge.

"Hurrah for Kenny!" cheered his crew mates and they gobbled it down.

"Join us," spluttered Gingerbeard, with his mouth full.

"Not in a million years," said Mario.

"Yes, and I'm not very hungry either," said Cosmo.

However, the Admiral decided to join them, and he and Gingerbeard swapped stories about their daring adventures on the high seas.

Once the meal was over and
the stories had been told, and
some rum had been drunk and
some arm-wrestling had been
done, the ghost pirates and their
lost-and-found shipmate said a
happy farewell. They sang a
haunting song as they slowly faded
into space.

Cosmo, Mario and the Admiral
went to the window and watched as

the dark ship creaked and rose into
the air until it was lost in the cold
night sky.

"Here's to a fine captain and
crew," said the Admiral, swinging
up his hand in salute, "and a first-
class chef."

6. Back at Base

Cosmo crossed Cuthbert Road car park and knocked on the hatchway of Mr Pringle's shed, the HQ of the Pricklebourne League of Paranormal Investigation.

Mr Pringle opened it and popped his head out.

"Ah, Cosmo," he said. "Did you manage to sort out the groaning?"

"Yes, Mr P," said Cosmo.

"And did it involve ghosts of any kind?" asked Mr Pringle.

"Oh, yes," said Cosmo. "Pirates and a ghostly ship and a love story from centuries past."

"Excellent!" said Mr Pringle. "Come in and tell me all about it."

"Not tonight, Mr P," said Cosmo, yawning. "I'm a bit tired." Then he handed Mr Pringle a flat box. "Pizza. A present from Mario."

"My word!" exclaimed Mr Pringle, licking his lips. "It certainly has been a successful mission. See you later then. Oh, and well done." And with that he disappeared back into his shed.

Cosmo had just about reached the other end of the car park when he heard a muffled cry from the shed. The hatchway opened and Mr Pringle stuck out his head.

"Anchovies!" he yelled. "Cosmo, I hate anchovies!"

"There's no pleasing some people," yelled Cosmo, and he ran off home for his supper.